Angels FC

Awesome Attacking

Suffering Substitutes

Crafty Coaching

Michael Coleman

illustrated by Nick Abadzis

D1585792

ISBN 9798644482771
Publication & Format © Michael Coleman 2020

Text © Michael Coleman as dated below, 2020
Illustrations © Nick Abadzis as dated below

Email: admin@michael-coleman.co.uk
Website: www.michael-coleman.co.uk

for

Bob Jeffreys

The three titles in this volume were originally published by
Orchard Books, 338 Euston Road, London NW1 3BH
as follows -

Awesome Attacking, Suffering Substitutes, Crafty Coaching
in a three story bindup format:
2004, paperback, ISBN 1-84362-239-4
2008, paperback, ISBN 978-1-40830-011-4

Awesome Attacking as an individual volume:
1999, hardback, ISBN 1-86039-933-9
2000, paperback, ISBN 1-86039-934-7
text © Michael Coleman, illustrations © Nick Abadzis

Suffering Substitutes as an individual volume:
2000, hardback, ISBN 1-86039-937-1
2001, paperback, ISBN 1-86039-938-X
text © Michael Coleman, illustrations © Nick Abadzis

Crafty Coaching as an individual volume:
2000, hardback, ISBN 1-84121-509-0
2001, paperback, ISBN 1-84121-511-2
text © Michael Coleman, illustrations © Nick Abadzis

Angels FC

CONTENTS

An Angels FC Story

AWESOME ATTACKING

Michael Coleman

illustrated by Nick Abadzis

1

Football Fan-Atic

"Jon-jo Ri-ix! There's only one Jon-jo Ri-ix!"

"Your mum's in good voice again, Jonjo," laughed Colly Flower as the two Angels strikers warmed up for the start of their match against Jubilee FC.

Out on the touchline, waving her Angels scarf and singing her head off, was Mrs Rix.

Jonjo groaned. "Don't mention it! Talk about embarrassing. I sometimes wish she was like our Carla."

Sitting on the ground near the warbling Mrs Rix was Jonjo's younger sister, Carla. As usual she was lost in a book about boarding schools and midnight feasts.

"What, not interested in football you mean?" said Colly.

"No," sighed Jonjo. "Miles away!"

But Mrs Rix was very much there - as everyone realised the moment the game began. For until then, just like the Angels players, Mrs Rix had been merely warming up.

"Go-go, Jon-jo! Go-go, Jon-jo!" she chanted as Jonjo brought a good save out of Jubilee's goalkeeper with a dipping long shot.

"'Ere we go, Jon-jo-jo, 'ere we go!" she sang when her son rose to meet one of Mick Ryall's corner kicks and just scraped the bar with his header.

And a mazy dribble, in which Jonjo beat three Jubilee defenders and hammered another shot narrowly wide, actually sent Mrs Rix into rhyme:

It was too much. The next time the ball went out for a throw, Jonjo hurried across.

"Mum, be quiet!" he pleaded. But he was wasting his breath. Ten minutes before half time, when Jonjo raced through on his own to drill a low shot into the corner of the net and put Angels 1-0 up, Mrs Rix went totally wild.

"Yahooooo! Goal-y! Goal-y, Gooooaaaaaal!" she screamed, leaping into the air before racing onto the pitch to plant a huge kiss on Jonjo's forehead and cry, "That's my boy!!"

All around him Jonjo could hear the other players giggling. Finally managing to break free from his mum, he scurried back to the centre circle. Rhoda O'Neill met him with a big grin and a moistened hand.

"Let me wipe the lipstick off, Jonjo! Pink doesn't go with the Angels' colours!"

Jonjo blushed to the roots. Go? At that moment there was only one thing he wished would go - his Mum!

And then, just before half-time, she did. As the singing and chanting suddenly stopped, Jonjo glanced hopefully across to the touchline.

Had his Mum swallowed a fly or something equally wonderful? No, she hadn't. With a book-free Carla actually running to catch her up, Mrs Rix was heading towards a battered old caravan standing in the far corner of the Angels ground.

The Angels' coach, Trevor Rowe, had acquired the caravan when he first arrived as vicar of St Jude's Church. He had been offered it by one of his parishioners. Most people would have turned the old heap down, but not Trev. He'd had it painted in club colours and turned it into a mobile refreshment hut!

And, even though Trev had often talked about replacing it with something newer, the caravan was still in use. The parents all took it in turns to open up and sell drinks and sweets to the spectators at half-time and today it was obviously Mrs Rix's turn.

"Well done everybody," said Trev, as the Angels gathered at the side of the pitch during the interval. "You're all playing well. Any injuries?"

"I've got a problem with my left ear," said Bazza Watts with a frown.

Trev looked concerned. "Why, what have you done to it?"

"Got it too close to Jonjo's mum," laughed Bazza. "But I'll be all right, Trev. I'll be on the far side of the pitch this half!"

"Thanks for the warning, Bazza," said Tarlock Bhasin, the Angels' other wing back. He pulled his turban low down over his ears. "I'd nearly forgotten I'll be that side!"

Jonjo winced with embarrassment. What wouldn't he give for a quiet second half!

No chance. The best he'd get would be a quiet opening five minutes while his mum cleared up in the caravan. Perhaps he could make the most of it and bang in another goal while she wasn't looking!

But after Jonjo's sparkling first-half performance, the Jubilee manager had obviously given his team instructions to watch him carefully. So when, shortly after the restart, Lennie Gould put him through with a brilliant defence-splitting pass, the Jubilee goal-keeper was alert to the danger.

Coming quickly off his line, he raced out and dived on the ball a fraction of a second before Jonjo reached it. Unable to stop himself, the Angels' player flew over the goalkeeper's body and landed on the ground.

"Foul! Penalty!" somebody screeched instantly. Jonjo looked up. It was his mum, dashing across from the caravan. Behind her, Carla was ambling back to her book, a bar of chocolate in one hand and a bottle of pop in the other.

The referee, who was well up with the game, shook his head firmly. "No foul! Well saved the keeper! Play on!"

The Jubilee goalkeeper thumped the ball upfield. Behind him Jonjo found that he'd got a problem. He reached down towards his ankle.

Seeing this, Mrs Rix wound herself up to top volume. "My boy's injured, referee! Stop the game!"

The referee looked carefully down at Jonjo. Then, clearly happy, he ran off.

This was too much for Mrs Rix. As the referee scampered upfield to follow the play, Jonjo's mum dashed on to the pitch to follow the referee!

"I said stop the game!" she yelled in his ear, "My boy is injured! He might have a broken leg!"

And with that she grabbed the referee's whistle, nearly strangling the poor man with his own cord, and put it to her lips.

Peeeeeeeeeep!!

Play stopped at once. Releasing the gasping referee, Mrs Rix raced back to the penalty area. Jonjo was now moaning and holding his head in his hands.

"Jonjo!" exclaimed Mrs Rix. "Tell Mummy! Where does it hurt? Do you want me to call an ambulance?"

"No, I don't!" screamed Jonjo. "It doesn't hurt at all!"

"Doesn't hurt? Then … then, why are you sitting on the ground?"

"Because, when I fell over their goalie my boot came off. I was just putting it back on again!"

2

It's For You-Hoo!

It was a silent journey home. After his
Mum's outburst Jonjo hadn't played at all
well and, in the end, Angels had been
lucky to win 1-0.

"Oh, how
embarrassing," said
Mrs Rix finally.

"You can say that
again!" snarled Jonjo.

Mrs Rix opened the
front door and hurried inside. "I mean,
why couldn't you have waved your boot
or something? Anything to show that you

weren't badly injured and stop me making such a fool of myself." She shuddered. "Goodness knows what that referee must have thought of me."

"Everybody knows what he thought of you, Mum!" howled Jonjo. "He showed a red card! You were sent off!"

Jonjo flopped into a chair. The shame of it! Having your own mum sent off! If that had happened to him, he'd have earned at least a one match ban ...

A ban? Jonjo began to wonder. Would his Mum be banned? The referee had certainly yelled something about reporting her as he'd waved his red card.

The thought of his Mum missing a match suddenly seemed very attractive. In fact, after what had happened, maybe she would feel the same?

"Er … I don't suppose you'll want to come and watch next week, will you? Not after what happened …"

Mrs Rix snorted. "What! Let a silly misunderstanding like today's put me off? Never! We think going to your games is wonderful, don't we Carla?"

Jonjo's sister, her face still smeared with chocolate, looked up from her book. "Awfully super!" she said, to Jonjo's great surprise.

Jonjo trudged miserably upstairs to his room. By the look of it, the only thing that could keep his mum off the touchline would be an official letter from the Chairman of the Junior League Committee saying she was banned!

An official letter? Maybe he could write one on the school's computer! No, that was no good. He'd need some official Junior League notepaper to make a letter look right.

Sighing, Jonjo looked out of his bedroom window … only to break into a wide grin as his gaze settled on the phone box standing right outside their front gate.

He wouldn't need notepaper for a telephone call!

He waited until Monday evening. As soon as it got dark, Jonjo announced, "I'm going upstairs to do my homework."

Once in his room he put a chair against the door - then opened the window and climbed out. A quick slide down the drain pipe, a vault over the gate and he was in the phone box!

He'd got it all worked out. He would put on a deep voice and say that he was Mr Bilgrami, Chairman of the Junior League committee. He would say that the Committee had studied the referee's report - and they'd decided his mum should be banned from watching the next Angels game!

Pushing his money into the slot, Jonjo dialled their own telephone number. The ringing lasted for a few seconds until a squawky voice answered.

"Hello! Carla Rix speaking!"

Jonjo groaned. It was his sister! "I want to speak to Mum ... er, I mean, can I speak to your mum, please?"

"No."

"What do you mean, *no*?" exploded Jonjo, almost forgetting to disguise his voice.

"She's not here. Hang on, I'll get my big brother."

Jonjo gulped. Her big brother? She meant him! As the line went quiet, Jonjo shot out of the phone box, over the gate, up the drain pipe and back into his bedroom. Carla was already banging on the door.

"Telephone," she was shouting. "Somebody for Mum."

Jonjo snatched opened the door. "Well, why didn't you get her then?"

On the other side of the landing the bathroom door was sharply yanked open by a dripping Mrs Rix, a towel wrapped round her. "Because I said I was going to have a nice long soak and didn't want to be disturbed! But now I'm out," she grumbled, "I might as well talk to whoever it is."

As she headed down the stairs, with Carla close behind, Jonjo slammed his bedroom door shut. Out of the window he went again, down the drain pipe, over the gate, and back to the phone box. Even before he got there, he could hear his mum's voice crackling.

"Hello! Hello! Mrs Rix speaking! Is anybody there?"

Jonjo snatched up the receiver. "Yes!" he puffed, trying to get his breath back and sound like a serious adult all at once. "My name is - gasp! - Mr Bumgrimly ... I mean, Bilgrami! I am Chairman of the Youth Football League Committee ..."

"Well this had better be good, Mr Bilgrami. I'm standing in a puddle of water for your benefit!"

Jonjo made it as snappy as he could considering he'd got hardly any breath left.

"Mrs Rix, my Committee has just met and I am calling to say that we take an extremely dim view of our referees being assaulted. We have decided to impose a one match ban on you."

There was a short silence from the other end before Mrs Rix said simply, "Oh. I see."

"You will not be allowed to watch Angels play Framley Flyers this Saturday," added Jonjo, thinking maybe he should spell it out.

"Oh," said his mum again.

"But you can watch the game after that," added Jonjo, sensing her disappointment. "Goodbye!"

For the final time Jonjo raced back along his route. But this time he needn't have hurried. As he came back down the stairs and into the lounge it was obvious that his mum hadn't moved since he'd said goodbye to her. She was still holding the phone and looking stunned.

"That was a League official. I've been given a one game touchline ban."

Jonjo did his best to look surprised. "Oh, Mum. You mean you can't come and watch me on Saturday? What bad luck. It won't be the same without you and Carla there."

A sudden wail came from near the window. "But that's awful," cried Carla. "I jolly well *want* to go!"

"But I'm not allowed, dear. And you're not old enough to go on your own."

"I'm nearly seven!" retorted Carla. "That's awfully old! In my books, girls get sent away to boarding school at that age!" she added, stamping her foot for good measure. "I want to go to football with Jonjo!"

Jonjo was expecting his Mum to squash this idea at once. But instead Mrs Rix said, "Well ... I suppose it isn't far ... and there aren't any roads to cross ..."

"And I'll have Jonjo to look after me," added Carla quickly.

"What!" cried Jonjo. "I don't want you tagging along with me!"

"Yes, you do," said Mrs Rix. "You just said it wouldn't be the same without us."

"I know, but ..."

"Well, at least if Carla's with you it won't seem quite so bad, will it?" Mrs Rix looked thoughtful. "I know. Carla, you can go to training with Jonjo tomorrow. If that works out all right, then you can go to the game with him on Saturday. How does that sound?"

Carla gave the sweetest of smiles.

"That sounds awfully super! Doesn't it, Jonjo?"

"Awfully super?" muttered Jonjo through clenched teeth. "More like superly awful."

3

A Jolly Silly Game!

"I didn't know you liked football so much, Carla," said Jonjo grimly as they walked the short distance to the Angels' training session the following evening.

"I don't," said Carla firmly. "Football is a jolly silly game."

"What?" frowned Jonjo.

"Awfully silly. They don't play football in my books. They have midnight feasts and jolly exciting adventures."

Jonjo exploded. "Then why make so much fuss about coming with me if you don't like football?"

"Because I *do* like chocolate and pop!" said Carla, breaking into a jig. "They have chocolate and pop at midnight feasts!"

So that was the reason Carla always came to watch his games, even though she was bored. To get her half-time treat and pretend she was one of the soppy girls in her soppy stories!

As they arrived outside the changing rooms, Jonjo irritably put his sister straight. "Well you're out of luck this evening, Carla. This is a practice session. The caravan isn't open."

"Not open?" Carla's face fell.

"That's right. No chocolate, no pop!"
Jonjo pretended to cry. "I'm jolly sad about
that, can't you see? Boo-hoo!"

Carla watched her brother disappear
into the changing room. "You *will* be sad,
Jonjo Rix," she said, her eyes glittering.
"Just you wait and see ..."

As the training session got under way,
Jonjo checked to see where Carla was.
Seeing her sitting, book in hand, beside

Trev's big holdall, and the rest of the team's training equipment, he gave a satisfied nod. Firmness, that's all it had needed. Show her who's boss.

But Carla didn't stay still for long. The moment Trev began to put the Angels through their paces with jogging and sprinting exercises, she started looking for what she needed. By the time the Angels stopped for a drink before their practice game, she was ready.

"We're playing Framley Flyers on Saturday," Trev told the squad as they gulped down water from their squeezy bottles, "and they like to play the offside trap. So, Jonjo, I want you to fool them by drifting out to the wing until Lennie or Rhoda play a long ball over their defender's heads. Then you race across. I want to see some awesome attacking!"

"Awesome attacking!" grinned Jonjo. "I like it!"

And so it was that Jonjo, drifting out to the wing as instructed, found himself very close to where Carla was sitting, reading her book. In midfield, Lennie Gould ran forward with the ball. Hitting just the sort of through ball Trev had described, he yelled, "Go, Jonjo!"

Jonjo sprinted off - only to stop dead as a jet of water hit him smack in the eye!

"I said go," bawled Lennie, "not stay!"

Jonjo swung round to see where the water had come from. But all he saw was Carla, still gazing intently at her book.

The next through ball for Jonjo came a couple of minutes later, a defence-splitting pass from Rhoda O'Neill.

"Go, Jonjo!" she screamed.

Again, Jonjo raced off - and again he slithered to a halt, this time as a jet of water blasted him in the ear! He swung angrily round to look at his sister.

"Are you firing water at me, Carla?" he demanded.

"Me?" said Carla. "I'm reading, can't you see?" She looked innocently up at the sky. "Maybe it was a pigeon," she said sweetly.

The strain was getting to Jonjo. When Lennie hit another through ball for him, he paused, half-expecting to be hit by another spurt of water. When nothing happened, Jonjo sprinted off - only to screech to a halt once again as he heard the sharp peep of a whistle!

"What did you stop for?" called Trev, refereeing from the middle of the pitch.

"I heard you blow your whistle!"

"I didn't. You must be hearing things!"

Jonjo swung round. "Carla, did you peep just then?"

His sister smiled sweetly. "Of course I did! I peeped at my book!"

And so it went on. After twenty minutes of squirts and whistles, and whistles and squirts, Jonjo didn't know whether he was coming or going.

"One more try, Jonjo!" called Trev. "Concentrate!"

Rhoda hit another great through pass. Jonjo set off. Again, a whistle sounded. Determined to keep going this time, Jonjo swung round to look towards Trev but didn't stop. As he did so, a squirt a water hit him in the back of the neck! Totally confused, Jonjo swung round again. What was going on?

He saw at once. Satisfied that she'd given Jonjo enough trouble, Carla let her book fall to reveal what she'd been hiding behind it ever since she found them: a squeezy water bottle, and a referee's whistle from Trev's holdall!

The effect was dramatic. Not knowing whether to continue chasing the through ball or run back to thump Carla, Jonjo found his head going one way and his feet going the other. Careering off the pitch, he planted his foot in the bucket of water, tripped, and ploughed head-first into the pile of practice footballs!

"Awesome attacking?" said Lennie Gould as the team gathered round. "More like awful attacking, Jonjo!"

Jonjo trudged away from the training session, a picture of misery. It had been the worst evening of his entire life.

"Just wait till we get home," he snarled at Carla. "When I tell Mum about you, she won't let you come anywhere near my football match on Saturday!"

His sister looked up at him and simply shook her head. "You tell about me, Jonjo, and I'll jolly well tell about you. You and your *mysterious happening*."

"What are you on about?"

"Like in my stories. They always have *mysterious happenings*. So, when I saw you slide down the drainpipe and run to the phone box the other night, I thought: a *mysterious happening*! I'll have to tell Mum about that!"

"You didn't … you didn't tell her?" gulped Jonjo.

Carla shook her head. "Not yet. But if I don't get the biggest bottle of pop and the biggest bar of chocolate on Saturday …"

Jonjo knew when he was beaten. "All right, all right," he sighed. "You'll get them."

4

Midnight Feast

It had been a rash promise. Jonjo didn't want to spend his pocket money buying Carla the smallest bottle of pop and bar of chocolate, let alone the biggest. But if he went back on his promise, he'd be in trouble. She'd either tell on him, or plague him with tricks that would turn him into an awful attacker again. Probably both!

The girl was a total menace. As far as Jonjo could see, the only time she was perfectly safe was when she was asleep.

Asleep …

Jonjo thought about it. What if, come Saturday, Carla was too tired to watch the match? Even better, what if she was fast asleep when the time came for him to leave?

Was that likely? His sister went to bed early and was usually up before the milkman. A grin spread slowly across Jonjo's face. But what would happen if she didn't get much sleep on Friday night …?

Jonjo moved slowly up the stairs, anxious not to drop the heavy tray he was carrying. Padding across the landing, he backed into Carla's tiny room. By the light of the moon he put the tray down on the floor, then bent to whisper in his sister's ear.

"Carla! Wake up! Look what I've brought you!"

Carla sat up in bed, yawning and blinking. "I thought we'd have a midnight feast!" Jonjo went on. "Just me and you. Like they have in your books."

"Super!" nodded Carla, her eyes becoming almost as round and bright as the moon peering through her window when she

saw the overflowing tray that Jonjo was handing to her. On it were mounds of salt and vinegar crisps, stacks of peanut butter sandwiches, piles of biscuits - and that was just the top layer! Jonjo had heaped on everything he'd been able to find.

"You have some too, Jonjo" mumbled Carla through a mouthful of crisps.

"No, it's all for you."

"You have some, too!" insisted Carla, her voice rising. "Nobody in my books has a midnight feast on their own!"

Jonjo quickly grabbed a couple of crisps to keep her quiet. "All right! But you've got to eat the rest because … because … I'm going to tell you a story!"

Carla's mention of her books had given him a sudden flash of inspiration. He could keep his sister awake even longer by telling her a story - a blood-curdling story that would make her too frightened to close her eyes!

"It's a story about a jolly mysterious boarding school," Jonjo began.

"Why? What was mysterious about it?"

"The head teacher was an enormous giant with hands that could crush bones into dust and teeth that were as sharp as a shark's ..."

"Golly!" gasped Carla. "Did he like midnight feasts?"

"He certainly did," said Jonjo in his most sinister whisper, "and his favourite food was a hot, steaming pie made from little girls ..."

"That was a funny story," giggled Carla when Jonjo finally ran out of blood-curdling ideas at two o'clock in the morning. "Tell it to me again, Jonjo!"

By three o'clock, the food had all gone. "I want some seconds!" said Carla. Jonjo crept downstairs to refill the empty tray. "Tell me another story," said Carla at four o'clock.

At five o'clock, she yawned, then said, "All that food has made me jolly thirsty!" Once again Jonjo crept downstairs, to fetch a glass of water.

"Now I need to go to the loo!" Carla chirped at six o'clock. "And when I come back, I want to hear that giant head teacher story again!"

At seven o'clock, she said nothing.

Instead she slipped silently out of bed and trotted off downstairs to turn on the television.

In the bedroom Jonjo was stretched out on the floor. He gave a sigh, a big yawn … and seconds later he was sleeping like a baby …

5

What A Load Of Rubbish!

"Jonjo! Jonjo! Wake up!"

Jonjo jerked his eyes open to find his mum shaking him by the shoulder. "Wha-what time is it?"

"Nine o'clock! Your match kicks off in an hour! I thought you were getting ready until Carla came down and told me you fell asleep reading her a story."

"Carla?" mumbled Jonjo. "You mean she's *not* asleep?"

A wickedly smiling face popped out from behind Mrs Rix. "No fear! I can't wait to go to the match! Hurrah!"

Jonjo couldn't believe it. His sister was looking as lively as ever - while he felt awful!

Blearily he got his kit together and off they went, Carla skipping merrily at his side. "Chocolate and pop!" she trilled, "chocolate and pop! I'll never stop loving chocolate and pop!"

Jonjo checked the coins in his pocket and sighed. Not only did he have no energy, he'd soon have no money. Buying

Carla enough chocolate and pop to keep her quiet was going to take every penny he had!

And then, as they reached the Angels' ground, he saw it. Somebody had scrawled 'CLOSED – CARAVAN SOLD' across the side of the caravan.

His sister had seen it too. "Closed?" she scowled.

Jonjo groaned. "It's not my fault! Trev must have sold it at last!"

"No chocolate and no pop *again*?" Carla's voice was as icy as the look in her eye. "Then I'll just have to be an awful lot more awful than I was before …"

"No!" cried Jonjo, panic-stricken. "I'll get you something, somehow. Just wait there. And don't do anything till I get back!"

Diving into the changing rooms he put on his Angels kit in record time. If he was quick, he could dash off to the shop down the road and be back before kick-off. Racing outside, he hurried towards the caravan to tell Carla what he was going to do.

But she was nowhere to be seen. Only when he reached the caravan itself did he spot her. Her late night had finally got to her. She'd climbed inside and stretched out on one of the long seats. She was fast asleep!

What was more, after having no sleep all night Carla probably wouldn't wake up until the game was over!

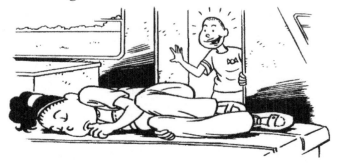

Jonjo tip-toed away. He was Carla-free at last!

But, as the teams lined up, Jonjo soon realised that now he had something else to worry about. He just couldn't stop yawning!

He yawned as the whistle blew to start the game. He yawned as Colly Flower kicked off and tapped the ball to him. And he was still yawning as the Framley Flyers striker darted in and took the ball off his toe.

"Wake up, Jonjo!" yelled Lennie Gould.

Jonjo tried to do just that. He shook his head. He slapped himself on the face. He pinched himself hard. None of it did any good, and it was all he could do to summon up enough energy to drift out to the wing as Trev wanted.

After ten minutes play, Rhoda O'Neill won the ball. Seeing Jonjo in position, she hammered a superb pass over the top of the Flyers' defence.

"Go, Jonjo!" she yelled.

Jonjo set off. But his legs felt so wooden they might have been chair legs. Before he'd got anywhere near the ball, a Flyers' defender had overtaken him and put the ball into touch.

Not long after, the Flyers won a corner. Jonjo trudged back to help out in defence. Taking up a position on the Angels' goal line, he leaned against a goal post. He yawned. His eyes drooped.

Slowly he felt himself sinking into a deep, delicious sleep … until he woke with a start as the corner was taken and a fierce shot from the Flyers' striker hit him on the head and bounced to safety!

"Good stop, Jonjo!" yelled Kirsten. "Now get back upfield!"

Jonjo groaned. Not only did he feel dead tired, he now had a headache as well! All he wanted to do was join Carla in the caravan and have a good snooze.

And so it went on, throughout the first half and into the second. Getting wearier by the minute, Jonjo hardly had a kick. Whenever Trev's tactic was tried and a through ball was played for him, he was either too late setting off or too slow to reach it.

Finally, with the score still at 0 - 0, he saw the referee look at his watch. Great! Any minute now he'd be blowing his whistle for the end of the game. Jonjo would be able to go straight home to bed. Assuming he could wake Carla up, that was. The lucky thing was probably still snoring her head off.

Enviously, he glanced over at the caravan – and blinked. Something wasn't quite right, he was sure. What was it?

Jonjo racked his weary brain. Was it the 'Sold' notice on the caravan's side? No, that had been there when they arrived. Then what was different?

Suddenly it came to him. The caravan had been standing still before – and now it was moving!

But how? A-ha! Even with a brain like cotton wool, he could work out the answer to that. It was because that big lorry in front of the caravan was starting to tow it away. Jonjo peered at the sign on the side of the lorry. What did it say? "The Crushing Crew. Scrap Merchants."

Jonjo couldn't have woken up faster if he'd been thrown under a cold shower. Scrap Merchants? The Crushing Crew?

Trev must have sold the caravan for scrap! But Carla was still inside! His book-mad, clever, screechy, funny, pain-in-the-neck, loveable-really sister was about to be squashed into a little cube. He had to save her!

Lennie Gould must have spotted what was going on too. From behind him, Jonjo heard him shout, "Go, Jonjo!"

Jonjo didn't need telling twice. As the lorry jerked towards the gate, he began sprinting down the pitch at blinding speed. He had to get to that lorry!

Suddenly a football flew over his shoulder and landed right in his path. Jonjo lashed it out of the way with his left foot, not slowing for an instant.

On he went, sprinting even faster as he heard the loud shouts and screams of encouragement coming from the other Angels players. On and on until, just as the lorry was about to turn out of the gate, he slithered up to the driver's door and banged on his window to make him stop.

Moments later he'd raced back to the caravan and opened the door - only to find Carla wide awake and looking as though she'd been enjoying every minute.

"Hurrah!" cried Carla. "Jonjo to the rescue! What a super adventure! Much better than chocolates and pop! Well done, Jonjo!"

Adventure? She thought he'd arranged the whole thing, realised Jonjo, just like the midnight feast! Hugging her with relief, he started to explain. "It wasn't well done really, Carla ..."

"It jolly well was," retorted Carla, pointing across to the pitch. "Ask your friends! They think so too!"

With cries of "Well done, Jonjo!", every Angels player was racing towards him! What was more, the Flyers' goalkeeper was picking the ball out of his net and the referee was blowing for full time!

"What a tactic!" cried Colly Flower, steaming up.

"Fantastic through ball from me," crowed Lennie. "And for once you moved when I shouted, Jonjo!"

Through ball? Shout? Slowly it dawned on Jonjo that Lennie might not have been shouting at him because of the caravan, but because he was about to try another through pass. That's why the ball had

flown over his shoulder as he ran! And what had he done to the ball?

"Unbelievable shot, Jonjo," cried Rhoda O'Neill. "Their goalie didn't see it!"

He'd hammered that ball anywhere just to get it out of his way - and it must have gone into the net!

Angels had won 1 - 0 … and he'd scored the goal of the season by accident!

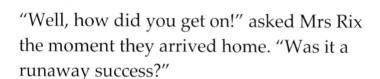

"Well, how did you get on!" asked Mrs Rix the moment they arrived home. "Was it a runaway success?"

"Very nearly!" giggled Carla.

"We won 1 - 0," said an exhausted Jonjo, already dreaming of his bed.

"Oh, I wish I'd been there," said Mrs Rix.

Jonjo stopped at the foot of the stairs. "Never mind, Mum," Jonjo yawned. "You will be next week."

As far as he was concerned, his Mum could embarrass him as often as she liked, just so long as never again did he have to go through the torture of looking after his sister.

But Mrs Rix simply said, "No, I won't. This came after you left this morning."

She was waving an important-looking letter. Jonjo could make out the Junior Football League crest at the top. What was going on?

"That silly person who rang me up got his dates all wrong," Mrs Rix went on. "I wasn't banned from going to today's match at all. I'm banned from watching next week's."

Jonjo couldn't believe it. His mum had received an official ban after all. He looked at Carla and gulped. "But – that means …"

"We can have even more awfully super adventures, Jonjo!" squealed Carla. "Hurrah!"

An Angels FC Story

SUFFERING

SUBSTITUTES

Michael Coleman

illustrated by Nick Abadzis

1

Muscle Man ...

"Coo-ee! Lion-el!!"

Lionel Murgatroyd's head turned slowly, but beneath his white gymnast's vest his heart was racing like an Olympic sprinter with his shorts on fire.

Nikki Sharpe, the most gorgeous girl in the gymnastics club, was heading his way!

"V- Vello, Hikki!" stammered Lionel.

"Pardon?"

Lionel struggled to get his tongue under control. "I mean, hello Veggie. No! I don't mean that! I mean Nikki! That's it. Hello, Nikki!"

"Hello, Lionel," purred Lionel's dream girl.

She was holding a clip-board and carrying a pen between her slim fingers. Thrusting both into Lionel's trembling hands she asked, "Will you be the first person to sponsor me, Lionel? Per-leaaase?"

Lionel's stomach did a backwards somersault. Sign her sponsorship form? He'd walk across a beam strewn with banana skins if she asked him to! Taking the pen, Lionel signed his name with a flourish. Only then did he wonder exactly what he'd signed. He looked at the printed section at the top of the form.

WALKING THE TIGHTROPE

I will be walking a tightrope
to raise money for the
Dudmanton Charity Fayre !
Please sponsor me for
as much as you can afford.

Lionel gulped. How much could he afford? Was Nikki Sharpe as good at tightrope-walking as she was at making his knees turn to jelly?

"How - er, how far do you think you'll get?"

"Oh, no more than four or five metres. I'm no good at it, really. You'd be much better. I've seen you walking on the beam. You're wonderful."

"Vanks merry thatch," gurgled Lionel. "I mean, thanks very much."

"You're so steady," cooed Nikki. She bent down and gave Lionel's knees a little squeeze. "I wish my legs were as strong as yours ...Muscle Man!"

Muscle Man? Lionel quickly put himself down for 25p a metre before he fainted with delight.

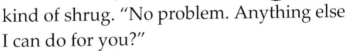

"Ooooh, thank you, Lionel!"

Lionel gave what he hoped was a muscle-y kind of shrug. "No problem. Anything else I can do for you?"

"Well ..." Nikki Sharpe's eyelids fluttered. "A little birdie tells me you play football for Angels F.C. You couldn't get the whole team to sponsor me, could you?"

"Sure! Leave it with me! I'll get them all signed up." Even if I have to pay the money myself! thought Lionel.

Nikki Sharpe sighed. "I love football! And I bet you're really good at it, aren't you, Lionel? Just like gymnastics."

Lionel bit his tongue. Much as he'd like to say it, he *wasn't* good at football. Gymnastics was his best sport. He could trot along the narrow beam as if it was a wide street. But play football?

Football was different. Lionel loved the game, loved everything about being part of the Angels FC squad – but a good footballer he wasn't. He couldn't run very fast, he couldn't tackle very hard and, worst of all, when Lionel kicked a ball it always shot off in the strangest directions.

That was what he should tell Nikki Sharpe. But, as he gazed into her deep blue eyes, he just couldn't bring himself to admit it.

Instead he said, "I'm … er … not *bad* at football …"

Which is true, thought Lionel. Sometimes I'm not bad. Sometimes I'm terrible.

But Nikki Sharpe clearly wasn't convinced. "I think you're being a modest Muscle Man," she cooed. "I think you're really the best player in the Angels team. I bet you're near enough out on your own."

"Ah. Now that *is* near enough true," said Lionel.

It was, too. While the rest of the squad were playing on the pitch, he would be standing on the touchline along with Ricky King, the Angels' other substitute. If that wasn't being near enough out on his own, he didn't know what was!

"Admit it, Lionel. You're their top player, aren't you?"

"Well," cried Lionel, truthfully again, "I've never been substituted!"

"A star footballer!" sighed Nikki Sharpe. "And a super star Muscle Man for getting your less talented team-mates to

sign my form!" She took Lionel's quivering hand in hers. "You will come to the Fayre on Saturday and watch me walk the tightrope, won't you Lionel? Per-leaase!"

Lionel nodded furiously. "White rope talk at the hair on fatter day? Yes! Yes!"

Lionel couldn't wait until the next training session to get Nikki's form signed. Instead he took it with him on Sunday evening to the St Jude's Youth Club. All the Angels team were members.

"Ricky!" he called, seeing Ricky King the moment he stepped through the door. "Just the man to sponsor a tightrope walk."

"Sure, Li," said Ricky, signing the form at once. "Say, how long have you been a tightrope walker?"

Lionel looked down at the form. Nikki had forgotten to put her name at the top. He was about to say as much when he thought better of it. He would get the form signed a lot quicker if he didn't have to explain that he was doing it for a girl whose tinkling voice gave him goosepimples on his goosepimples.

"How long have I been a tightrope walker?" he said. "Er … not long."

Off he went around the room. He'd just managed to get the final signature when Trev, the Angels' coach, bustled in. "Attention, everybody!" he cried. "I've got some news about next Saturday's match."

Jeremy Emery frowned. "I didn't think we had one, Trev."

"We didn't," said Trev. "But we have now. I've just had a call inviting Angels FC to take part in a special friendly match against Royals FC."

The players exchanged excited glances. They'd heard that Royals FC were a good team, but had never met them before.

"It may be a friendly, but they're taking it seriously. I'm told they even had a spy at last week's match."

Lionel winced. The previous week, with Angels 4 - 0 ahead, he'd been sent on for the last ten minutes. By the time the final whistle blew they'd been pulled back to 4 - 3 and were hanging on by the skin of their teeth!

"Now I know it's short notice," Trev went on, "so is everybody available?"

Lionel looked round the room. For once he was pleased to see the nodding heads. It meant he wouldn't be needed …

"How about you, Lionel?" asked Trev. "I might need to call on you."

"Er …" began Lionel, wanting for once to say that he couldn't play - but definitely *not* wanting to say why! "I'm not sure, Trev. I kind of, er … promised to go to the Dudmanton Charity Fayre."

Trev grinned. "Then you *are* available, Lionel. That's where we're playing. The challenge match is one of the main attractions!"

At the Dudmanton Charity Fayre? The same Fayre that Nikki Sharpe would be at?

As the news sank in, Lionel's heart sank with it. A football-mad Nikki Sharpe would be bound to watch the match; and when she realised that one of the teams was Angels FC, she'd be bound to look for him; and when she saw that far from being their star player, he was only their substitute …

It was too awful to think about. She'd either laugh at him or else tell everybody what he'd said so that *they* laughed at him. One way or the other he'd be made to suffer. He'd be a suffering substitute!

No, decided Lionel. Somehow, he had to get himself into the starting line-up.

The question was - how?

2

… Or Banana Man?

The obvious way to get picked was to turn in a brilliant performance at training. If he did that, Trev might put him straight in the team for Saturday's match against Royals FC

So, it was a determined Lionel who handed Nikki Sharpe her completed sponsorship form at the gym club on Monday evening …

"Thank you, Lionel!" she cooed. "You're my little twinkling star!"

… And an even more determined Lionel who turned up for training on Tuesday.

After their warm-up exercises and skills sessions, he elbowed his way between Colly Flower and Jonjo Rix to kick off for the Angels' usual practice match.

"Hang on, Lionel," said Colly. "I'm striker, not you. You usually play … er, *where* do you usually play?"

"Everywhere," said Lionel. "That's half the problem. I need to find my best position. I think it might be striker."

Too kind to tell Lionel that he'd be surprised if he could strike a match, let alone a football, Colly trotted back into midfield.

More than that, when he won the ball from Rhoda O'Neill a few minutes later, he slid a perfect pass through to where Lionel was loitering, slap-bang in the centre of the penalty area. It was a golden chance for him to score.

"Aim for the bottom corner, Lionel!" Colly shouted encouragingly.

Lionel looked up at the goal, looked down at the ball, looked up at the goal again, picked his spot - and shot.

Wwwhhhhhhhhhheeeeeeeeeeeeee!

The shot whizzed off his boot like a rocket - but, sadly, a rocket without a rudder. Heading straight for just a fraction of second, it then began to curve away from the goal ... and away ... and away ... until, with a clatter, it smacked the corner flag out of the ground!

"I think Colly meant the corner of the goal, Lionel," shouted Jonjo, trying not to laugh. "Not the corner of the pitch."

Lionel sighed. Maybe striker wasn't the position for him after all. Maybe midfield was the place for him to be, spraying brilliant passes in all directions.

"OK, change over," he told Colly. "I'll play centre midfield, you be striker. And get ready for some special passes!"

Lionel's chance came as Daisy Higgins won a tackle and swept the ball to him. He saw at once that, up ahead Colly was in bags of space.

"Get ready, Colly!" yelled Lionel, lashing the ball forward. "Here it comes!"

But, once again, almost as soon as it started, the ball began to curve wildly to the right … and curve … and curve … until this time it knocked the centre-line flag out of the ground!

"Not quite a defence-splitting pass, Lionel," called Daisy. "More of a flag-splitting pass!"

Lionel scuttled up to her. "Maybe I'm really a defender. How about doing a swap?"

Daisy agreed, and back went Lionel into the heart of defence. Easy, he decided. With everybody except goalkeeper Kirsten Browne in front of him, even his worst pass would have to go near somebody!

He was wrong.

The next time the ball came near him was when Lennie Gould, playing on the other side, swept through the middle only to be stopped by a last-ditch tackle from Jeremy Emery.

"Kick it into touch!" called Jeremy, as the ball bobbled free.

"Mine!" yelled Lionel.

Racing across he tried to hammer the ball away - only to see, yet again, the ball curve off to the right as if it was a rocket-powered banana and begin shooting towards his own goal!

Only a wonderful save from Kirsten Browne stopped it from going into the net.

Lionel sank to his knees in despair. Out

on the touchline Trev was jotting something down in his notebook and Lionel had a good idea what it was:

"Do NOT pick Lionel Murgatroyd, even if it means Angels take the field with only ten players!"

And so it was a stunned Lionel who was pulled to one side by Trev after training was over and told, "Lionel, you're in the team for Saturday."

Lionel's mouth fell open. "Wha- wha- what did you say?"

"I said you're in the team for Saturday," repeated Trev. "Mick Ryall will be substitute instead of you.

Trev shook his head as he walked away, muttering mysteriously, "Sending me a petition. I hope they know what they're doing."

Petition? wondered Lionel. What was Trev on about? Lionel was too ecstatic to care.

He was in the team!

Lionel did a handspring. He did a somersault. He did a handspring-y kind of somersault with a treble twist and perfect landing. He was in the team, and Nikki Sharpe would see him play like ...

Oh, no, realised Lionel. Nikki Sharpe would see him play like he usually played – hopelessly! Completely and utterly hopelessly!

And *that* would be even more humiliating than having her find out he was only a suffering substitute instead of a super star.

Now he didn't want to be in the team after all!

3

It's Not Fayre!

A gloomy Lionel, sports bag over his shoulder, who drifted through the gates of the Dudmanton Charity Fayre at 2pm on Saturday afternoon. Hard as it had been, he'd come to a decision. He was going to tell Nikki Sharpe the truth about how useless he really was at football.

Off he went to search for her, hardly noticing the crowds as he pushed through them - and certainly not noticing Trev slip out from behind a tree and start to follow him.

Lionel had just reached some sort of football sideshow when he saw Nikki hurrying his way.

"Coo-ee! Lionel! I hear Angels FC are playing at the Fayre today! Oh, I can't wait to see my Muscle Man star in action!"

It was just the opening Lionel needed. "Er … look, Nikki. You've what it gong … I mean, you've got it wrong."

"Got what wrong?"

"About me being the Angels' star player." Lionel took a deep breath - then blurted out the truth. "I'm not a star. I'm hopeless, in fact. Useless. Totally, totally, useless."

He finished with a sigh then, shame-faced, looked down at the ground. There, he'd said it. But what would Nikki Sharpe say to him in return? Lionel was ready for a screech of anger, or a howl of rage. But not the silvery giggle he heard.

"Oh, Lionel you can't fool me. Useless, indeed! You're just being modest; I know you are!"

Modest? Modest? Suddenly it sank in. *She didn't believe him!*

"But I *am* useless! I can't play football for toffee!"

How could he convince her? A sudden shout from the nearby football sideshow came to his rescue.

"Roll up, roll up! Flatten the goalie and win a prize!"

The sideshow consisted of a goal - and a wooden goalkeeper on a stand. The idea was to hammer a penalty straight and true so as to knock the goalie over. What's more, Mick Ryall was about to try his luck. Perfect!

"Mick! Let me have a go first, eh?"

"Definitely," grinned Mick, standing to one side. "This I've got to see!"

Lionel turned to a bemused Nikki Sharpe. "This will prove it to you. A chimpanzee with a broken toe could do this better than me. I'm so useless I'll miss that goalie by a mile!"

No, thought Lionel as he got ready to take his shot. I'll make it even more convincing. I'll use my left foot. Then I'll miss by two miles!

He stepped back. He ran in. He hit the ball. Off it flew, perfectly straight … and stayed straight! Without swerving by as much as a centimetre, it smacked against the wooden goalie and rebounded like a cannonball - straight into Mick Ryall as he stood watching!

"Ohhhh," groaned Mick, collapsing in a heap at the horrified Lionel's feet.

As Trev appeared – from nowhere, it seemed to Lionel – to administer first-aid, Nikki Sharpe seemed almost as stunned as Mick.

"Fan ... er ... tastic, Lionel! You ... you *are* a star. Didn't I say so!"

Trev gave Nikki a quizzical look, before turning back to the groaning Mick. "No game for you today, Mick," he said. "Not even as a substitute."

Now what do I do? thought the suffering Lionel. Nikki Sharpe didn't believe him and Mick Ryall couldn't take his usual place in the team even if he'd wanted to. *How could he get out of the game?*

"I hope Ricky's here," Trev was saying. "We won't have a substitute if he's not."

Ricky! That was it. He would find Ricky and ask him to play instead. Then Lionel could go back to being substitute. If Nikki Sharpe asked why, he'd pretend to have injured himself tripping over a candyfloss or something.

"Are you coming to watch me tightrope walk then?" asked Nikki.

"Yeah, but … er … I've just got to do something first. I'll catch you up!"

Leaving a frowning Nikki Sharpe to go her own way, Lionel hurried off in search of Ricky King.

He found him fifteen minutes later – or, rather, Ricky found him.

"Li! Here, man! You're just the dude I need!"

Ricky was standing near another football sideshow called *Three-Legged Shoot-Out*.

"Be my partner, Li!" urged Ricky before Lionel could say a word. "We've got to tie our legs together, y'know, three-legged style, then dribble a ball down and bang it into the net. Quickest time today wins the prize."

Lionel looked at him in amazement. "And you want *me* to be your partner? Mis-kicker Murgatroyd?"

"Sure, I do. You're a gymnast, man! Running in a straight line and keeping your balance is easy for you."

"Kicking the ball straight isn't."

Ricky waved away the objection. "I'll do that bit. You just run."

Seconds later he'd handed over his money and a man had strapped Lionel's right leg to Ricky's left. A ball was put in front of them – and they were off!

"Go for it, Li!" yelled Ricky as they spurted across the ground in perfect co-ordination, "we've got this sewn up!"

On they went, up to the penalty area, the ball still at Ricky's right foot.

"Hit it!" yelled Lionel.

"I can't!" screamed Ricky. The ball, hitting a bump in the ground, had bobbled away from him and in front of Lionel. "You hit it!"

Lionel didn't have time to think. The ball was in front of him. But his right leg was attached to Ricky's left.

There was only one thing to do. For the second time that day he smacked in a shot with his left foot ... and, strangely, for the second time that day, he hit as straight, as true, as rocket-like a shot as any player had ever hit before. In the blink of an eye the ball screamed into the net, catapulted back out again – and promptly clobbered Ricky!

Yet again, Trev was miraculously nearby. He dashed over, helped revive the crumpled Ricky, but then confirmed Lionel's worst fears.

"Ricky's out of action too. He's going to have a bump on his head the size of an egg. A dinosaur's egg."

"You mean …" began Lionel.

Trev nodded. "Yes, we're down to eleven fit players. You'd have been playing anyway." He looked hard at Lionel. "That petition wasn't needed."

Petition? thought a confused Lionel. What was Trev on about?

He couldn't hang around to find out. He'd run out of people to take his place in the team. There was only one thing left to do.

Lionel hurried off towards the Dudmanton Charity Fayre Tightrope Challenge. And so, a short distance behind him, did Trev.

4

Don't Look Down!

Lionel's mind was made up. He didn't want to be in the team. Not only would he make a fool of himself in front of Nikki Sharpe but, even worse, he would let the rest of the side down. In fact, the more he thought about it the more he decided that the Angels would be better off playing with only ten players.

And ten players were what they would be left with if he got himself injured! After all, he'd accidentally injured both Mick and Ricky. Injuring himself on purpose should be easy! And what better way to do it than in front of Nikki Sharpe's very own eyes?

"Coo-ee! Lionel!" trilled the girl herself, appearing at his elbow the moment he reached the Tightrope Challenge. "I couldn't wait for you to arrive, so I've just had my go. Guess what happened!"

But Lionel wasn't interested in guessing. He was more interested in the quivering tightrope. Stretched between two high posts about ten metres apart, it was perfect! Take a nose-dive off that and he would definitely do himself a mischief!

Only then did he notice, to his dismay, that beneath the rope layers of soft, spongy matting had been put down for people to fall on to without hurting themselves. It wasn't fair! How could he hope to give himself a decent injury with those mats there?

At his elbow Nikki Sharpe was still talking, only less patiently. "Don't guess,

then. I'm going to tell you anyway. Look!"
She pointed at a small flag stuck in the
ground about five metres from the start of
the tightrope walk. "My marker! I'm in the
lead!"

"Great!" cried Lionel.

"Oh, enthusiasm at last."

But Lionel hadn't been enthusing over her performance. He'd just seen the solution to his problem. He needn't worry about the mats. All he had to do was tightrope walk as far as that nice pointy flag, then jump onto it. A hole in his foot would be sure to keep him out of the game!

Quickly, he handed over his money and climbed to the starting platform. "What are you doing?" cried Nikki Sharpe anxiously. "Get down. You've got a football match to play in."

"I don't want to play in it," Lionel shouted back. "They'll do better without me!"

And with that, he stepped out onto the rope.

It was just like being on the beam at gymnastics, only a bit thinner and more wobbly. But, holding his arms out wide, Lionel got himself nicely balanced - then off he went.

One metre. Three metres. Five metres!

He could see the pointed marker flag sticking up invitingly, all ready for him to jump on to …

"Keep going! You're the best so far!"

Lionel could have cried. The man in charge, who was following him along beneath the rope, had just plucked the flag out of the ground. It wasn't there to jump on to any more!

There was only one thing to do. The landing mats ended at the finishing pole. If he walked the whole length of the tightrope, he could launch himself off the end and onto the lovely patch of rock-hard ground beyond the mats. That should get him a broken ankle at least!

On he went. Eight metres. Ten metres. He was at the end of the rope! It was time to jump!

"Stop!" screamed a girl's voice nearby.

"Yaaaaahhhhhh!" yelled Lionel as he fell – only to land on the soft, comfortable mat Nikki Sharpe had managed to shove beneath him just in time!

Lionel was furious. But then so was Nikki. "You broke my record," she said with a scowl.

"Well, you broke my fall!" Lionel retorted angrily.

"Of course, I did! You could have hurt yourself and missed the match!"

"But I wanted to missed the match! I keep telling you. *I'm no good at football!*"

Nikki Sharpe's eyes glittered wickedly. "Tell me something I don't know," she said.

"What?"

"I know what you're like at football!" snarled Nikki Sharpe. "I spied on your last game, the one where you came on for the final ten minutes. That's when I came up with my petition plan to get you into the Angels team for today."

Lionel looked at her, mystified. "Petition plan? What petition plan? And why would you want me in the team anyway?"

"Because she plays for Royals FC, Lionel," said a familiar voice nearby.

Nikki Sharpe looked up at Trev and laughed nastily. "Too right! And with Miskicker Murgatroyd here playing for your lot we're definitely going to win!"

5

Lionel Lines Up

Stunned, Lionel watched Nikki hurry
away laughing.

"I don't understand," \
he said sadly.

"I think this will
explain it," said
Trev, holding out
a sheet of paper for
him to look at. "It
dropped through my
letter-box before training on Tuesday."

The sheet was covered in the signatures of the Angels' players. At the top it read:

We, the undersigned, reckon that Lionel Murgatroyd should be in the team for the match against Royals F.C.

Lionel Murgatroyd

So, this was the mysterious petition Trev had been on about, realised Lionel. The petition in Nikki Sharpe's plan!

"I thought it was genuine at first," said Trev. "That's why I put you in the team."

Lionel sighed. "But it was a forgery. What she needed was all the Angels signatures. She just pretended to like me so that I'd collect them all for her on her petition form."

"But Nikki made one big mistake. She forgot that you wouldn't have put your own name down first on a petition asking me to pick *you* for the team," said Trev. "When I looked more closely at it yesterday and saw your name right there at the top, I realised something fishy was going on. That's why I've been following you around all afternoon - to see if I could solve the mystery."

"And now you have," said Lionel, glumly. He looked down at his own feet. "She was right to want me in the team though, wasn't she? I *am* rubbish. She's right when she says they'll beat us with me playing."

Trev put his arm round Lionel's shoulders. "I don't think she is, Lionel. Not from what I've seen of you this afternoon. You've got talents I never knew you had."

"I have?" gasped Lionel. "What talents? What are they? Tell me, tell me, tell me!!"

Trev simply smiled. "I'd prefer you to discover them for yourself, Lionel. But here's a clue. You're playing on the left wing!"

Left wing? Lionel was still thinking as the match got under way. *What sort of a clue was that?*

Lionel hadn't the faintest idea what to do on the left wing. So, when Rhoda O'Neill played the ball out to him after five minutes, he turned inside and tried to hit a through pass for Colly Flower. But, as ever, the ball squirted off his right foot bending like a banana straight to a Royals player who was only stopped by a crunching tackle from Lennie Gould.

Not long after exactly the same thing happened again. An attempted pass straight across the half-way line curled in the air and only just reached Kirsten in the

Angels goal before the Royals striker could get to it.

"Keep it up, Lionel," Nikki Sharpe taunted, running past. "You're doing everything right - for us!"

Lionel was going to shout something back when he stopped in his tracks. What had she said? *You're doing everything right?*

Right? Suddenly the memories of that afternoon came flooding back. His *left-footed* penalty that had rebounded and whacked Mick Ryall. The *left-footed* shot that had rebounded and flattened Ricky King. Trev must have seen them both. Could that be why he'd put him out on the left wing?

He was still thinking about this as Tarlock Bhasin, receiving the ball from Kirsten, played it on down the line.

"Lionel!" screamed Jonjo Rix, running into a gap in the Royals defence, "Hit it!"

Lionel did just that. Stopping the ball with his right foot, he turned and struck it with his left. Ping! Without swerving by a single centimetre, Lionel's pass put Jonjo in the clear. All the Angels' striker had to do was race on and bang the ball past the Royals' goalkeeper to put Angels 1-0 ahead!

"Luck!" sneered Nikki Sharpe. "You won't do that again."

But Lionel did do it again. Again, and again. Across the field, down the wing, at all sorts of angles, Lionel's left-footed passes couldn't have gone straighter if they'd been world-champion homing pigeons.

Nikki was getting narked. As Lionel slid yet another left-footed pass just out of her reach mid-way through the second half she snapped, "Right! You *definitely* won't do that again."

Lionel laughed. "Don't you mean, '*Left*! I definitely won't … *Aaaaggghh!*"

With a scything tackle, Nikki Sharpe had charged in and cracked him hard on the left ankle.

While the referee gave her a stern lecture for the ferocious foul, Trev raced on and sloshed cold water over Lionel's ankle. By the time he'd finished Lionel was able to run again but the moment he tried to kick the ball with his left foot a fierce pain shot up his leg.

"Said you won't do that again, didn't I?" hissed Nikki Sharpe.

"Do you want to come off, Lionel?" called Trev.

Lionel refused. But soon he was wondering if he'd made a bad mistake. Unable to use his left foot, his game was back to its normal hopeless self.

An attempted pass inside to Lulu Squibb banana-ed away over Jeremy Emery's head and allowed the Royals' striker to run through and hit the ball past Kirsten. 1 - 1!

More right-footed passes went astray, the ball curving round like a boomerang every time he hit it with his right foot. It was awful. Every time Lionel got the ball the Angels ended up going backwards!

Soon, the whole team didn't dare venture forwards. Encouraged by this, Royals swept onto the attack leaving a miserable Lionel standing out on the left wing.

"Lionel!" It was Trev, moving towards him and pointing down at the white touchline. "That line is a gymnastics beam. Got it?"

He didn't get it, but Lionel nodded anyway. "For the last ten minutes of the match I want you to run up and down on it. Don't move off it at all."

Lionel nodded again, glumly. He knew what Trev was doing. With his one talent no longer working he was keeping him out of the action.

Or was he? Because Trev then added, "And listen for my instructions!"

So for the next few minutes Lionel trundled up and down the touchline as carefully as if it was as high off the ground as a real gymnastics bar. Meanwhile over on the rest of the pitch the Royals mounted attack after attack.

Then, with a superb interception, Daisy Higgins broke clear for the Angels. A swift pass forward found Lulu Squibb. She turned past her marker and clipped an angled ball on to Jonjo Rix … only for Jonjo to be heavily tackled himself. The ball squirted free, bobbling towards the touchline ahead of Lionel.

"Go, Lionel!" cried Trev. "But stay on the line!"

Lionel spurted forward, reaching the ball just as it was about to go out of play. Then, obeying Trev's instructions to the letter, he began to dribble the ball along the touchline.

Now Trev was running beside him. "Keep going Lionel, keep going …"

Lionel ran on. Soon he was almost level with the penalty area. What was Trev thinking of? Was he getting him to dribble the ball down to the corner flag to waste time?

It seemed he was. For, still running beside him, the Angels coach was shouting, "Now when I say, hit it as hard as you can straight at the corner flag! Wait for it, wait for it …"

Lionel dribbled and waited, dribbled and waited - until suddenly Trev screamed "Now!"

In a blur of movement, Lionel did what he'd been told. He looked up, took aim at the corner flag, and hammered the ball right-footed with all his might.

Off scorched the ball, bang on target –
until, as ever, it began to curve and curve
… away from the corner … across the
penalty area … over the head of the
Royals' goalkeeper … and into the net!

2 - 1 to Angels! And a goal to Lionel!

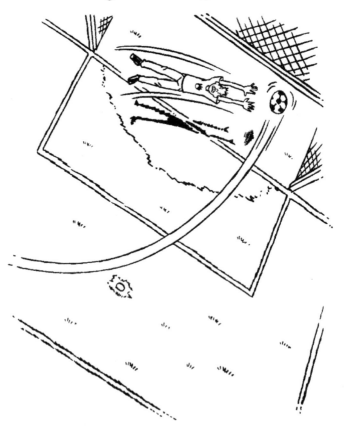

"Well done, super-sub," grinned Trev as the whistle went for full time. "Three prizes at the Fayre *and* a winning goal! Like I said, Lionel, you've got talents!"

"A great left foot," nodded Jeremy Emery enthusiastically.

"And an amazing banana shot from the left wing," laughed Lulu Squibb. "How on earth did you work that one out, Trev?"

The coach smiled. "Simple, really. Whenever Lionel aimed at the goal, he'd hit the corner flag – so I thought if I encouraged him to aim at the corner flag he'd hit the goal!"

"And he did! Two talents found in one day," said Jonjo Rix.

Bazza Watts pointed. "But one girl lost, by the look of it."

A scowling Nikki Sharpe had collared Lionel and was obviously telling him what she thought of him. Finally, she turned around and flounced away, her nose in the air.

"She called me a rotten cheat," said Lionel. "Said I'd only pretended to be hopeless and that anybody who could do banana shots like that had to be half a Brazilian at least!"

"So, no more Nikki," said Bazza Watts. "Are you suffering from a broken heart?

Lionel's face split into a wide grin. "Nah. She was starting to drive me round the bend!"

An Angels FC Story

CRAFTY

COACHING

Michael Coleman

illustrated by Nick Abadzis

1

The Angels' Code

Peeeeeeeeeeeeeeeeeeeeeeeppp!!!!!

As the piercing sound cut across their training pitch, the whole Angels squad forgot about football and dived for cover with their hands over their ears.

"Wh- what was that?" mumbled Jeremy Emery, when the sound had finally faded away. "A rocket?"

"A jet fighter. Nothing less," said Tarlock Bhasin.

It was Kirsten Browne who was brave enough to put her head out from beneath her goalkeeper's jersey and see the real cause. "It was Trev! Look! He's over there."

The Angels coach was sitting in his car, a small suitcase on the seat beside him. "Sorry to frighten you, gang. I've been practising my whistling."

"That was a whistle?" said Lionel Murgatroyd. "It sounded more like a train entering a tunnel. How do you do that?"

"It's easy," said Trev. "My brother showed me. You press two fingers on your tongue and …"

"No!!" the Angels shouted as one, covering their ears. Trev laughed, then started the engine of his car.

"Off to your brother's farm are you, Trev?" said Tarlock glumly. "Again."

Trev nodded. "Afraid so, Lennie. I know having your coach missing isn't the best way to prepare for the new season, but my brother needs me more than the Angels at the moment. He's got flocks of sheep that need tending and he can't do that from his sick bed."

"Will he be better soon?" asked Daisy Higgins.

"He has to rest for a few more days," said Trev. "So, in the meantime, Lennie will take charge of the training sessions – starting this morning, Lennie."

Lennie Gould, the Angels captain, stood up a little straighter. "Okay, Trev. Anything in particular you want us to practise?"

Trev grinned. "Only one thing. The Angels Code. One, two, three …"

"Angels on and off the pitch!" chanted the whole squad in unison.

"Brilliant," Trev shouted out of his car window as he moved off. "Always remember that, and you won't go far wrong."

They watched him go. "Come on then, everybody," sighed Lennie. "Let's practise being Angels!"

They tried to act as if Trev really had been there with them. After some warm-up exercises, then spells of shooting and dribbling, they picked sides for a practice match.

Just as they were about to begin, though, they heard the fierce roar of a powerful motorcycle, and right up to the side of the pitch rode a huge man clad in leather. He pulled off his crash helmet. "The name's Wally Sly," he called.

"What an ugly mug," hissed Rhoda O'Neill. "He looked better with his helmet on!"

Wally Sly looked them up and down. "So," he growled, "you're Saint Trev's goody-goodies Angels FC, are you? I'm told you lot all behave nearly as perfectly as he always did."

"Always did?" echoed Lennie. "You mean … you've seen Trev play?" They'd often heard rumours that Trev was a good player.

"You could say that," snapped Sly. "It was awful. And I just can't believe he's coached a whole team to be like him – not a *successful* team, anyway."

Lennie gathered everybody together. "Right, let's show Slimy Sly how good a coach Trev is," he winked. "Bags of skill. And, just for fun, why don't we be *extra* angelic … ?"

They began their practice game. Almost at once, Jonjo Rix won the ball and put his striking partner Colly Flower through.

Racing to the edge of the penalty area, Colly hit a real whistler which was heading straight for the bottom corner of the goal – until Kirsten dived across and tipped it round the post!

"Ow!" Kirsten pretended to complain, sucking her fingers. "Hit it a bit softer next time, Colly!"

Colly immediately hurried up, looking as anxious as he could. "Oh, I'm truly sorry, Kirsten. Let me rub it better!" From the touchline, Wally Sly roared with anger. "Rub it better? You should be threatening to break it next time!"

The game continued. Speedy Ricky King got the ball and set off at a blistering pace. Unable to keep up with him, Daisy Higgins pretended to grab Ricky's shirt – only to angelically let it go again.

"Sorry, Ricky!" she trilled sweetly. "You're too fast for me."

Ricky stopped dead. "No, no, I'm the one who's sorry, Daisy. Shall I wait for you to catch up?"

"What!" screamed Wally Sly. "You should be telling her she's as slow as a slug and scooting past her every chance you get!"

Then he turned his attention to Daisy. "And you should be pulling his shirt right off!" he hollered, fists clenched, "and his shorts as well if that's what it takes to stop him!"

"Trev wouldn't like that," said Daisy, shaking her head solemnly and trying not to laugh.

"Then he's as crummy a coach as I expected," scoffed Wally Sly.

And so it went on, with the Angels players apologising for every little thing, simply so that they could make Wally Sly jump up and down in a fury. And then, just before the end of the session, it all went wrong …

Lulu Squibb was put through on goal. Racing across, Bazza Watts mistimed his tackle and sent fiery Lulu flying. She was back on her feet at once, her eyes blazing.

"You big banana!" yelled Lulu, "do you know what I'm going to do to you?"

Wally Sly was overjoyed. "At last!" he yelled. "Go on, belt him! Flatten him! That's what you're going to do, isn't it?"

Lulu stopped. That was exactly what she *had* been thinking. She might well have done it too, if Wally Sly had kept quiet. But now ...

"I'll tell you what I'm going to do to you, Bazza," she smiled through gritted teeth, "I'm going to give you a chance to say sorry for that tackle."

"Lulu, I'm sorry for that tackle," apologised Bazza at once, falling to his knees and polishing her boots with the sleeve of his shirt. "Forgive me!"

"Forgive you!" bawled Wally Sly. "I'd mangle every one of you! Call yourselves a football team? I could coach a team that would wipe the floor with you lot!"

The Angels had heard quite enough. "Why don't you, then?" cried Colly.

"We could do with an easy warm-up game before the season starts!" scoffed Rhoda.

"Then you'll see that Angels FC are coached by a winner!" shouted Mick Ryall.

Hearing this, Wally Sly smiled nastily … and thoughtfully … and very, very slyly. "So … supposing I did get a team together to play the Angels … you would expect the Angels coach to be the winning coach?"

They all walked straight into the trap. As the rest of the Angels nodded

enthusiastically in agreement Lennie

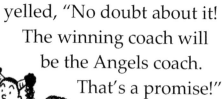

yelled, "No doubt about it! The winning coach will be the Angels coach. That's a promise!"

"Excellent!" said Wally Sly, triumphantly. "Then I *will* raise a team. And when they beat you, the winning coach will be the Angels coach. Me!"

"But – but –" stammered Lennie, realising what he'd been tricked into saying, "I didn't mean …"

"Of course you meant it," said Sly, pulling on his helmet and revving up his motorbike. "You promised!"

Trev returned just in time for the Sunday Club Night. All the Angels players were members of St Jude's Youth Club, which Trev organised as vicar of St Jude's Church. They told him at once about Wally Sly's challenge – but, before they could mention any more, a motorcycle roared up outside. Seconds later, Wally Sly was barging his way through the door.

Trev smiled and held out a hand. "Mr Sly! Welcome! Good to see you again!"

The Angels exchanged glances. It was true. Trev and Wally Sly had met before. So, were they friends? That question was answered immediately. No, they weren't!

"The name's Wally," snarled Wally Sly. "Big Wally. And you can keep your welcome. Have they told you about the challenge match they promised to play?" Trev nodded. "Then just say you agree to it as well."

"Of course," said Trev. "If my team have made a promise, then that's it. Angels keep their promises. We'll be there."

"Excellent!" beamed Wally Sly. "So, you'll be keeping the second part of the promise as well?"

Trev frowned. "The second part?"

Wally Sly glared at Lennie. "You haven't told him, have you? That's not very angelic, is it? Maybe you've forgotten what you did promise. Just as well I had this tucked

under my leather jacket then, wasn't it?"

And with that, Sly pulled out a portable tape recorder. He pressed the 'play' button and immediately Lennie's voice came out loud and clear:

"No doubt about it! The winning coach will be the Angels' coach. And that's a promise!"

Trev looked stunned. So stunned that, when Wally Sly said, "Agreed? The winning coach becomes the Angels coach!" and held out his hand, all Trev could do was shake it and seal Lennie's promise.

Lennie found the courage to speak up. "He won't win, Trev! We'll thump his team good and proper!"

Wally Sly guffawed. "Will you now? Well I'll be coaching my team on the corner pitch in the park tomorrow evening. Come and watch us – if you're brave enough!"

"And, er … what is the name of your team?" asked Trev quietly.

"Villains United," growled Wally Sly. "And I do mean villains!"

2

The Villains' Code

"S- sorry, Trev," stammered Lennie after Wally Sly had roared off on his motorbike. The other Angels said the same.

Trev shook his head. "Don't worry. He tricked me too. We'll just have to show him that trickery doesn't pay. I've done it once before ..."

The Angels coach disappeared before returning with a scrapbook. He flipped over the pages to reveal a yellowing newspaper cutting.

Sly-ding To Disaster!

The Amateur Cup Final at Wembley ended in complete humiliation for full-back Wally Sly yesterday. Given the run-around all afternoon by Trevor Rowe, who simply smiled and played on whenever he was fouled, Sly launched himself into a last-minute sliding tackle. But Rowe saw it coming. He stopped and, to the delight of the packed crowd, Sly slid on to demolish the advertising boards surrounding the pitch while Rowe raced away to score the winning goal...

"Wow! No wonder he doesn't like you," said Lennie. "You gave him the run-around and he's never forgotten it!"

"So how are we going to do the same this time, Trev?" said Colly, confident that their coach had a trick up his sleeve.

But Trev's face simply clouded over. "I don't know, Colly."

"He's not thinking straight," said Lulu as Trev drifted off. "He's worried about his brother – and now this."

"Then we'll have to help him," said Lennie. "We caused the trouble."

"Fine. What are we going to do first?" asked Daisy.

"First," said Lennie, "we're going to spy on Sly!"

The corner pitch in the park was near a clump of trees and bushes. The next evening, behind every tree and bush there squatted an Angels player.

"Wally Sly hasn't made a very good start," hissed Lennie. "They haven't put up the goals on this pitch yet!"

"Bang goes shooting practice then," said Kirsten. "Unless Wally is going to have his strikers aiming for his mouth!"

"Too easy," laughed Jonjo. "They couldn't miss!"

Tarlock pointed across the park. In the distance the large figure of Wally Sly was heading their way, his team trooping behind.

Colly hooted. "Look! They haven't even got a football with them! What's he going to coach them in – conjuring goals out of thin air!"

It was a good joke, so Colly was surprised when nobody laughed. Then he saw why. Wally Sly's players had drawn near enough to be recognised – and the others had realised this challenge match was going to be no joke at all.

"He's got Hacker Haynes in his team," gasped Lennie. "The dirtiest player I've ever met!" [1]

"And Zippy Larkin," groaned Daisy. "Who chases racing cars for a hobby. He hates me." [2]

Mick Ryall goggled unhappily. "There's Bruiser Bloor! He'll be after busting my glasses again." [3]

---

[1] See *Dirty Defending!*
[2] See *Frightful Fouls!*
[3] See *Dazzling Dribbling!*

Behind his bush, Lionel was shaking like a leaf. "Look, even Nikki Sharpe's playing for them. She'll be after me for sure!"[4]

"That's why they haven't got a ball," groaned Ricky. "They'll be spending so much time kicking us they won't have time to kick the ball as well!"

Out on the pitch, Wally Sly had gathered his team together.

"Right, you Villains," shouted Sly, shaking his fists, "who wants to wallop Angels FC?"

---

[4] See *Suffering Substitutes*

A forest of hands shot up. "We all do!" yelled Hacker Haynes. "We've all been made to look stupid by them. We want revenge!!"

"And so do I," growled Sly fiercely. "I once had thousands of spectators laugh at me because of Saint Trev. Now I'm going to get my own back. I'm going to be the Angels coach and take his team away from him."

"But won't he just start up another team?" asked Nikki Sharpe.

"He can't, it's too late. The season's about to begin! We'll become Angels FC instead. Won't the other teams get a shock! While they're expecting us to be all goody-goody, we'll trample all over them and win everything!" Sly glared around at his players. "Just so long as you lot win this match."

"That's the problem, ennit?" scowled Bruiser Bloor. "None of us have ever played for a team that's beaten the Angels."

"Well you haven't had me coaching you before, have you?" snarled Sly. "Someone who can use your fouling talents to the full! Now, let's get started!"

Behind the trees and shrubs, the Angels watched, horrified, as Wally Sly coached the Villains in how to shirt-pull, ankle-tap, body-check and foot-stamp without being spotted by the referee.

"So, remember the Villains' Code," snarled Sly at the end of the session. "Villains all over the pitch!"

The Angels crept out from their hiding places shocked and shaking. Mick Ryall stammered, "Wh- what are we going to do?"

"Rely on Trev," said Lulu firmly. "I bet he'll come up with a tactic at tomorrow night's training session."

Lennie coughed. "Er … Trev won't be there. He's gone off to help his brother again. He's asked me to run it."

"But we need a tactic," yelled Lulu. "Otherwise the Villains will mangle us!"

"Got any suggestions?" asked Jonjo.

"Yes, I have," Lulu snarled. "Forget the Angels' Code. Let's practise Wally Sly's tactics - the Villains' Code!"

3

Ouch!

At the following night's training session, they didn't bother with warming-up or shooting and dribbling exercises. Instead they went straight into a practice match.

"I don't want to hear anybody saying 'sorry'!" yelled Lennie, shaking his fist.

"Anybody who says 'sorry' to me," raged Lulu, "will be really sorry!"

They worked on shirt-pulling first. Bazza Watts and Mick Ryall were chosen to demonstrate. Mick dribbled mazily forward, but when he tried to race past Bazza the full-back reached out, grabbed a handful of Mick's shirt, and yanked him backwards. Except that, not being used to playing dirty, Bazza yanked too hard. Instead of simply slowing Mick down, he dragged him backwards – with the result that Mick elbowed Bazza in the ribs and had his own ankle squashed by Bazza's boot!

"Ow!" groaned Bazza, clutching his side. "Ooh!" moaned Mick, holding his ankle. "You two had better take a rest," said Lennie." But did everybody see how Bazza whacked Mick's ankle? Let's work on that!"

So, they tried an ankle-tapping session.

Collecting the ball in mid-field, Rhoda sprinted forward. Jeremy raced in at her from the right. Tarlock charged in from the left. Both were about to clout her on the ankles when Rhoda, realising that what was going to happen was going to hurt a lot, took fright – and stopped dead!

The result was chaos. Tarlock kicked Jeremy in the left ankle. Jeremy whacked Tarlock on the right shin. And, as they both hopped about in agony, they knocked Rhoda over and she crash-landed on her wrist!

"Ooh!" howled Jeremy.

"Eek!" gasped Tarlock.

"Agh!" screeched Rhoda.

Lennie groaned. "You three had better have a rest as well. Lulu and I will demonstrate making threats under our breath."

"Right," nodded Lulu. "I'll start."

She sidled up to Lennie and growled in his ear. "You big banana! Come near me and I'll give you a smack on the hooter."

Lennie snarled back, "You lumpy lemon! Touch me and I'll pull your ears off!"

Lulu turned and glared. "Pull my ears, you hairy horror, and I'll use your bonce as a football!"

"You pitiful prune!" shouted Lennie, getting carried away. "Do that and I'll tie a knot in your pigtails!"

"Oh yeah?" screeched Lulu, clenching her fists.

"Yeah!" bawled Lennie, his eyes popping.

Lulu poked Lennie in the chest. "Come on then, try it!"

Lennie twisted Lulu's nose. "Right, I will!"

And before anybody could stop them, they began fighting in a blur of arms and legs. The scrap could have gone on for hours if it hadn't been ended by the fierce and totally unexpected shriek of a whistle.

"It's Trev! He's back! His brother must be better!"

The Angels coach was standing on the far side of the ground, his fingers still in his mouth. Meekly the squad limped and hobbled their way across to him.

"Is this what you call being Angels?" he said bleakly.

"Trev, let us explain …" began Lennie. After they'd told him about the Villains team and their nasty tactics, Trev looked even more serious.

"Have you got a crafty tactic yet, Trev?" asked Ricky anxiously.

"No, I'm afraid I haven't."

"But you've got to think of something!" wailed Lionel. "If we lose this game you won't be the Angels' coach any more and we won't be Angels and … and …" His voice cracked and he buried his face in his shirt.

"Think, Trev. *Please*," urged Tarlock. "You've given Wally Sly the run-around before. You can do it again."

Trev suddenly brightened. "The run-around, eh?" he murmured. "Now there's a thought …" He turned on his heel and strode off.

"Where are you going?" called Jeremy.

"To invite Wally Sly to an extraordinary meeting in the Club Room tomorrow evening. See you all there!"

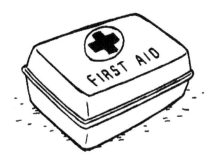

4

Bob Who?

The Club Room looked like a hospital's
Accident and Emergency Department.
Mick and Tarlock had bandaged ankles.
Jeremy had a lump on his shin. Rhoda was
nursing her bandaged wrist and, under his
shirt, Bazza was hiding his bandaged ribs.
As for Lennie and Lulu, they were covered
in so many bruises they'd lost count.

The door opened. Into the room stepped
a solemn-looking Trev followed by a
beaming Wally Sly.

"Oh dear," he chuckled nastily when he saw the wounded Angels. "What have you lot done to yourselves? You're not going to give my Villains much of a match, are you? Still, never mind. I won't be needing most of you when I take over as Angels coach. I don't have weaklings in my teams."

"You won't be taking over, Mr Sly," said Trev quietly. "I will still be the Angels' coach after this game because my Angels are going to beat your Villains."

Wally Sly snorted. "No chance! Saturday is going to be your unlucky day!"

"Luck will have nothing to do with it," said Trev, coolly. He paused, then added gently, "but if it does, then we'll have our lucky mascot to help us out."

"I didn't know we had a mascot," said Kirsten.

"Saturday will be his first appearance," said Trev. "His name's Bob. He lives with my brother on his farm." He glanced at Wally Sly. "I was wondering ... perhaps we could have a special rule, just for this

game. That mascots could play for their teams in the second half." Wally Sly looked suspicious. "How old is this Bob? How big is he? How good is he?"

Trev answered the three questions without hesitation. "Bob's four years old, he's about knee-high ... and he's never played football in his life before."

"And you want to bring him on? You must be desperate!"

"You agree then?" said Trev.

Wally Sly looked thoughtful. "Just so long as the Villains can bring on their lucky mascot as well."

Trev shook his hand. "Agreed. What's your mascot's name?"

"Wally," chuckled the Villains' coach gleefully. "Wally Sly. It's me!"

"But that's not fair!" cried the whole Angels squad.

"But nothing! It's was your coach's idea, not mine. He could have made himself your mascot, but he wasn't bright enough to think of that. So now you're stuck with little Bob." Wally guffawed loudly as he left. "See you on Saturday, then – with my biggest boots on!"

The Angels looked miserably at each other. Half of them were injured and in three days time they were going to be up against the meanest team that had ever been formed. As if that wasn't bad enough, Trev had just allowed himself to be tricked into allowing Wally Sly to come on for the Villains as well!

"I hope Bob is a four-year-old genius, Trev," said Bazza Watts. "When are we going to meet him?"

"Saturday," said Trev. "I'll bring him back with me that morning."

All around the room faces fell. "You mean," said Lennie, "you're going off again?"

Trev nodded. "I'm afraid so. My brother's much better, but it's a really busy time on the farm. The sheep all have to be brought in from the fields, and I'm not as experienced at it as he is. I'm improving, though ..."

But the Angels weren't listening. Trev's great tactic had turned out to be complete dud and they were going to get mangled by the Villains.

For the first time ever, not one of them was looking forward to playing their next match.

5

Angels v Villains

"Where's your coach, then?" sneered
Wally Sly as the Angels dawdled out on to
the pitch on Saturday morning. "Too
frightened to come and watch the
slaughter, is he?"

The Angels all looked desolate. They'd
been miserable before, but nothing
compared to how they felt now. Trev
hadn't arrived.

"He'll be here," retorted Lennie bravely.
"He must have been held up in the traffic."

"With little Bobby-wobby?" smirked
Wally Sly. "Ah, what a pity. Still we can't

wait for him. The game must go on." The
Villains coach ruffled Lennie's hair with
his huge paw. "Come on, look on the
bright side. It will all be over in an hour or
so."

He's right, thought Lennie gloomily.
That's just what it will be for the Angels –
all over.

The Villains had learned their lessons well.
The moment the match began, they were at
their meanest and sneakiest.

With only five minutes
gone, speedy Zippy
Larkin chased after a
through ball for the
Villains. But Daisy
Higgins had seen it
coming. Turning in
good time, she was
just about to kick the
ball safely into touch
when …

"How does this grab you, Daisy?" called Zippy Larkin – and, without the referee seeing, pulled her back by the shirt! Put out of her stride, Daisy could do nothing to stop him overtaking her and whacking the ball into the Angels net to put Villains 1-0 ahead!

Ten minutes later, disaster struck again. Mick Ryall got the ball in a crowded midfield. With the referee unsighted again,

in jumped Bruiser Bloor
– and down went
Mick, glasses flying
and clutching his
already injured
ankle. Worse, as
the ball ran free
Bloor played it
through for Zippy
Larkin to score again.

Angels 0, Villains 2!

"Didn't see that one coming, did you
four-eyes?" laughed Bruiser Bloor as Mick
limped off, to be replaced by substitute
Ricky King.

The Angels went on the attack. But in
another crowded midfield tussle, Hacker
Haynes elbowed Bazza in the ribs while
the referee wasn't looking, then whacked
the ball upfield for Zippy Larkin to outrun
Jeremy Emery and score yet again!

Angels 0, Villains 3 – and, with Bazza
also being too hurt to continue, on trotted

a very anxious Lionel Murgatroyd to replace him.

"We've just got to try to hang on until half time without letting in another goal," Lulu told him. "Maybe Trev will be here by then."

"Bang on till tough-time," stammered Lionel, tongue-tied with nerves. "KO."

Seeing this, Villains' Nikki Sharpe lost no time in whispering menacingly into Lionel's ear, "Coo-ee! Lionel! I'm going to kick yooouuu! Very haa-rrdd!"

The threat worked. When the ball came Lionel's way, he was quivering with fear so much that he didn't even notice he was facing his own goal. Desperately lashing out at the ball before Nikki Sharpe could get to him, Lionel could only look on horrified as it zoomed into the air, did a loop or two, then rocketed down past Kirsten and into the Angels net!

4 – 0 to Villains United at half time!

"Where's Trev?" moaned Colly as the shell-shocked Angels slumped on the ground. "We need him!"

"Here he comes!" whooped Lulu. Screeching his car to a halt, Trev ran to the back, lifted the tailgate – and out hopped a black-and-white sheep dog.

"What's this?" growled Wally Sly when Trev raced over with the dog trotting beside him.

"Our mascot," smiled Trev. "Bob. Four years old and no higher than your knee. And, as we agreed, I'd like him to play for the Angels in the second half."

"No chance," said Wally Sly. "Dogs are not allowed."

Trev sighed. "I see. Well, if you're going back on your promise, Mr Sly, I don't see why my players shouldn't go back on theirs …"

That made the Villains' coach change his mind very quickly. "All right, Bob can play for you! But …" Sly added slyly, "if he bares his teeth, then it counts as dangerous play, which is a yellow card offence. Right, Ref?"

The referee nodded in agreement, continuing to nod as Wally Sly went on, "Barking or snarling both count as ungentlemanly conduct and also get yellow cards. Two offences and Bob's sent off. And if he bites anyone, he's really in the dog house – he gets sent off straight away!"

"I agree," said Trev.

"And if he touches the ball with anything but his nose, then it's the same as handball," said Wally Sly.

"That's fine too," said Trev. "Bob won't be touching the ball." The Angels' mouths dropped open in surprise. "Won't be touching the ball?" gasped Bazza. "Then what *is* he going to do?"

"He's going to listen to my whistling," laughed Trev. "Now come on, Angels. Get out there and play your normal game!"

Still mystified, the Angels lined up for the start of the second half. And they grew even more mystified when Bob didn't join them, but simply laid down on the touchline close by Trev's feet.

But the moment the game restarted and Villains surged forward with Zippy Larkin on the ball, Trev gave a loud, long, low whistle. Off shot Bob, racing across the pitch! Without touching the ball, Bob raced back and forth in front of the Villains' player. Zippy Larkin found his way barred and had to screech to a halt.

"Foul, Ref!" bawled Wally Sly.

"Nonsense!" called the referee, "he's simply jockeying your player. All defenders do it. Perfectly legal!"

Trev whistled again. A short, sharp one this time. Bob instantly changed direction and began to steer Zippy Larkin back towards the centre circle. Hacker Haynes raced forward, calling for a pass. Trev whistled again – and Bob immediately switched his attention to race in front of Haynes as if he was herding sheep and Haynes was a runaway!

"Look!" cried Colly Flower. "Bob's bunching the Villains together as if they were a flock! They can't get near us to do their dirty tricks!"

Completely put off by Bob's antics, Zippy Larkin lost control of the ball. Tarlock nipped in and played it forward. Rhoda took it on. By the time she laid it into Jonjo's path on the edge of the Villains' penalty area, Bob had raced ahead and was rounding up their defenders into a little group. All Jonjo had to do was run forward and smash the ball into the Villains' net!

Within a few minutes, the Angels

had scored again. Colly scorched through on a run. Bruiser Bloor charged at him, ready to pull his shirt and tap his ankle for good measure. Trev whistled again. Instantly a black-and-white blur shot in front of Bloor to steer him away from Colly – who, now able to use his skill, ran on and planted the ball into the Villains' net to make it Angels 2, Villains 4!

"Bob's giving them the run-around," shouted Tarlock. "Just like Trev did to Wally Sly that time!"

"And Sly knows it!" yelled Jeremy. "Look, he's running away!"

It certainly seemed so. Furiously, the Villains' coach had jammed his crash helmet on his head, skidded out of the ground and was roaring off down the road.

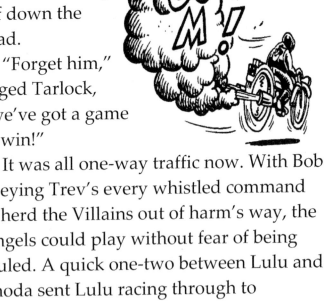

"Forget him," urged Tarlock, "we've got a game to win!"

It was all one-way traffic now. With Bob obeying Trev's every whistled command to herd the Villains out of harm's way, the Angels could play without fear of being fouled. A quick one-two between Lulu and Rhoda sent Lulu racing through to hammer in another goal for the Angels.

"Angels 3, Big Bananas 4!" screamed Lulu. "Let's score another one!"

The Angels mounted attack after attack. Rhoda scraped the bar with a rocket shot and Lennie came close with a looping header from one of Ricky King's long throws.

Then Lionel Murgatroyd got the ball on the halfway line. He dribbled forward, looking anxiously to one side as Nikki Sharpe charged in to tackle him – only to see her veer off in the opposite direction as Bob bounded up to protect him. Lionel dribbled on. Other Villains came towards him but couldn't get close to the ball as Bob circled round Lionel like a four-legged force field.

Lionel suddenly realised he was close to the Villains' goal. But how could he shoot with Bob dashing in front of him all the time? He needn't have worried. Trev had the situation under control. Two short, sharp whistles – and Bob instantly sat down at Lionel's side. All Lionel had to do was hammer the ball left-footed into the Villains' goal.

4 – 4 and still five minutes to go!

The Angels raced back to the centre circle. They were joined by Bob who immediately lay down on the halfway line, his ears pricked as he listened for Trev's next whistle. What he and everybody else heard instead, though, was the shattering roar of a motorcycle.

"It's Wally!" cheered the Villains. "He's back!"

Careering into the ground, Wally Sly skidded to a halt at the very edge of the pitch. "Ref!" he bellowed, "I'm coming on as my team's lucky mascot!"

Striding on to the pitch, the Villains' coach called his team together and muttered some instructions to them before they kicked off. When they did, Zippy Larkin, as instructed, passed the ball to Wally Sly – who promptly planted one heavy foot it, making it impossible for any of the Angels players to kick away.

Then he dug something out of his pocket and tossed it towards Bob. The sheepdog's nose twitched. He licked his lips. And then he began to gnaw.

"What have you given him?" cried Lulu.

"A tasty, roast bone," laughed Wally Sly. "I've just been to a pet shop to get it. Now you'll see some crafty coaching. Surround that dog, Villains!"

Before the Angels could move, the whole Villains team had raced forward, dropping to their knees to encircle the crunching Bob.

"Now keep him there," growled Sly, "until I put this on him!" Out of his pocket he pulled something else he'd bought from the pet shop – an ugly-looking chain and lead. Murmuring, "Good boy. Stay …" Wally Sly crept towards Bob. Closer and closer until, with Sly no more than a metre away, the air was split by the loudest, longest, shrillest, whistle Trev had ever produced.

Instantly Bob left his tasty bone, leaping high out from the circle of Villains as they tried to grab him. Desperately, Wally Sly dived headlong to try and stop Bob escaping – only to land on top of his own players!

"Aggh!" they all screamed as Wally Sly squashed them into the mud.

"The ball!" yelled Kirsten from her goal. "He's left the ball!"

She was right. In creeping forward to try to collar Bob, Wally Sly had taken his foot off the ball. It was free.

"Captain's ball!" screamed Lennie Gould joyfully.

And, leaving behind the whole Villains team as they struggled to free themselves

from beneath the vast shape of Wally Sly,
Lennie simply had to dribble the ball the
length of the field and tap it into the empty
Villains net.

Immediately there came another, very
different, whistle – the referee's, blowing
for full-time. Angels had won 5-4! The
whole team raced to surround Trev and
the tail-wagging Bob.

"Three cheers for Trev the Rev, our
crafty coach!" shouted Lennie.

"For ever and ever, amen!" yelled the others.

Trev smiled broadly. "Angels, you making coaching a pleasure. And that's something not all coaches are able to say. Ask Wally Sly!"

Out in the centre-circle, the Villains had freed themselves and were now angrily jumping up and down on their moaning, groaning coach.

"He doesn't seem to be enjoying his job, Trev," laughed Lennie.

"That's what happens when you're in charge of a team who don't play by the rules, Lennie," said Trev. "Coaching becomes a dog's life!"

Printed in Great Britain
by Amazon